Arabian Nights

Aladdin and the Magic Lamp

Indrani Vohra

Om KIDZ
An imprint of Om Books International

Long ago in Persia, lived a poor boy named Aladdin. He was a naughty boy who was always found creating chaos or playing with his friends. Aladdin's mother could only afford one meal a day, trying her best to fend for both of them, while Aladdin carelessly whiled away his time.

One fine day, while playing with his friends, Aladdin was visited by a big, burly man. He said to him, 'I am your uncle. It has been long since I visited you and your mother so I have come to see you two.'

Aladdin, taken aback, said, 'My mother never told me I had an uncle!' The man replied, 'You must ask her. She will tell you about me.' Aladdin went home and told his mother about the man he had met on the street. His mother said, 'Your father had mentioned his brother once. This man must be him.'

The man came visiting again and this time brought gifts for Aladdin. He said to Aladdin's mother, 'I know you have a hard life but I am here to help you. Let me take Aladdin along as I can get him some work.'

Thrilled to hear this, his mother instantly agreed and Aladdin set out on a magical adventure with his uncle.

While travelling across rivers and valleys, they suddenly saw a big rock. Aladdin's uncle stopped in front of it and called out, 'Oh mighty rock, open up and show us what you hold!' The rock parted to reveal an underground chamber. Aladdin was in awe. He thought to himself, 'My uncle is a magician!'

Aladdin's uncle told him 'Go down to the end of this chamber and you will find a room. Once there, search for a lamp and bring it to me.' He then pulled out a ring from his finger and handed it to Aladdin and said, 'Take this protective ring with you.'

Aladdin went down the opening nervously and reached the chamber filled with gems and treasures sparkling in the dim light. He looked around but couldn't find what he was looking for. He decided to fill his pockets with all the treasures and just when he was about to give up, he found lying in the corner, a shiny golden lamp! Holding the lamp, Aladdin went towards the opening.

He asked the magician to pull him out of the chamber but the magician insisted on being handed the lamp first. Aladdin realized that the magician had tricked him into doing this!

Aladdin was naughty but that also made him clever. He refused to give the lamp unless he was pulled out first. In anger, the magician closed the rock's opening. Poor Aladdin was stuck in the chamber! Disgruntled, he accidently rubbed the lamp he was holding.

All of a sudden, there was a loud thud and smoke began rising from the lamp. A genie emerged from the smoke! 'My master, I am the genie of the lamp and will appear whenever you rub your hands on it. How may I serve you?' the genie asked, introducing himself to Aladdin.

Aladdin was elated. 'Get me out of here,' he requested. 'Your wish is my command,' replied the genie and out came a flying carpet atop which sat both Aladdin and the genie as they flew passed the mountains and the desert sands. Soon they could see the city and its stunning palace on the horizon. Aladdin was home.

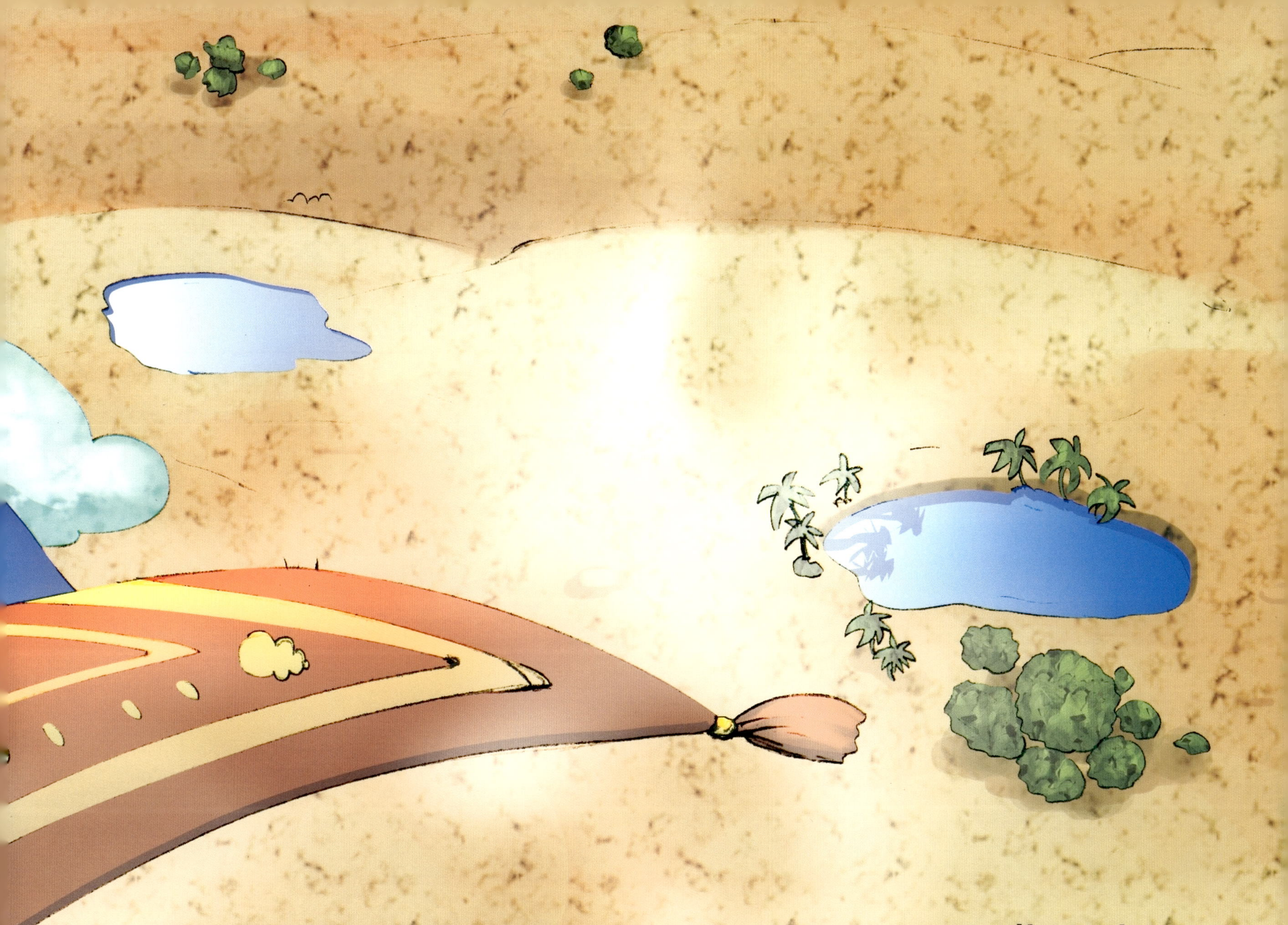

Aladdin hugged his mother, as soon as he saw her. He had missed her terribly and realised how much she meant to him. He related his adventures to his mother, telling her about how the man disguised as his uncle was actually a magician and had tricked them. He then told her about the genie while revealing the magic lamp which he had hidden in his clothes from prying eyes.

The whole adventure had left Aladdin tired and hungry. He asked his mother for food. Sadly, there was no food in the house. Once again, Aladdin rubbed the lamp and lo and behold, the genie appeared!

He asked the genie for some food and was presented with a beautifully laid out array of dishes for them to feast on! Aladdin was in the seventh heaven and ate to his heart's content.

Aladdin said to his mother, 'Now dear mother, all our troubles will vanish with this magic lamp and we will finally lead a comfortable life!' He hugged his mother who was moved to tears. Aladdin regretted being a careless, young fellow who had not been concerned about his mother. He promised himself that he would do all he could to make a happy life for them.

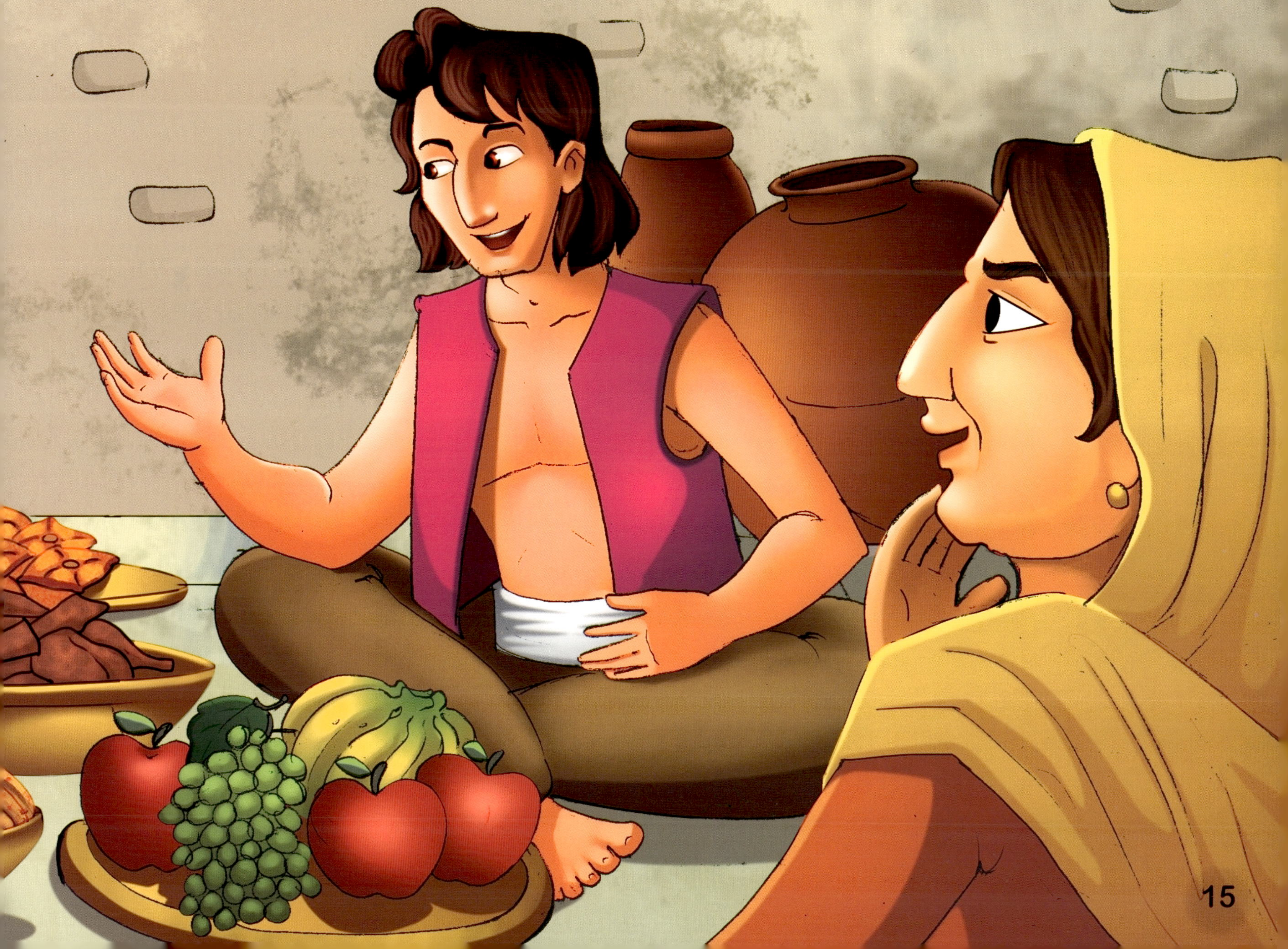

The magic lamp had helped him reunite with his mother, bringing all the happiness back. He used the magic lamp when he really needed it and helped out his mother more. From then on, Aladdin and his mother lived a happy and contented life.

Arabian Nights
Alibaba and the Forty Thieves

Indrani Vohra

Om KIDZ
An imprint of Om Books International

Once upon a time, in Persia, there lived two brothers–Kasim and Alibaba. While Kasim married the daughter of a rich merchant and ran a luxury shop, Alibaba married a poor woman and sold dry wood in the market.

One fine day, Alibaba was chopping wood when he saw a group of forty thieves on horses galloping towards him. He thought to himself, 'I must hide or they will kill me.' He climbed a tree and watched them ride towards a cave.

One of the men stood in front of the cave and said, 'Open Sesame,' and the cave magically opened. Alibaba was taken aback. After some time, the group emerged from the cave and another one of them said, 'Shut Sesame,' and the cave closed.

Alibaba thought to himself as he watched the thieves go, 'Why don't I try the magic words and enter the cave?' Standing in front of the cave he said, 'Open Sesame,' and watched the cave open. The cave was filled with jewels and riches which the thieves had stolen over the years!

Alibaba went back and told Kasim about the thieves. Kasim wanted to go to the cave and try his luck. But Alibaba warned him about the thieves. He didn't listen and went ahead anyway. He said the magical words and the cave opened to reveal the treasures to him. By now, the thieves were on

their way to the cave. They found Kasim inside the cave, filling bags with gold coins and treasures. They killed him instantly, leaving his body inside.

The next morning, Alibaba went looking for his brother and found his body inside the cave. He thought to himself, 'Oh Kasim, I had warned you!' He took his brother's body back and with the help of Marjenah, Kasim's loyal servant, gave him a burial.

On discovering that the body was missing from the cave, the forty thieves realised that someone knew their secret and decided to track him down. Through one of the villagers at Kasim's burial, the thieves discovered Alibaba!

Then, one day, one of the thieves found Alibaba's house. He put a cross mark on the house so that he could come back with other thieves later. That night, the forty thieves returned to the village. When they came, they found cross marks on all houses!

Smart Marjenah had seen the thief put the cross mark and proceeded to fool them this way. The thieves connived again. This time, their leader showed them jars filled with oil and said, 'I will dress up as an oil merchant and visit Alibaba. You will get inside these jars and when I signal to you by throwing stones, rush out of your jars and attack him.'

The leader visited Alibaba with forty jars, one filled with oil and the other thirty-nine, hiding the other thieves. He asked him for food and Alibaba invited him to dine with them. Marjenah discovered there was no oil in the house. So she thought of taking oil from the jars. As she opened the jar filled with oil, the thief inside the other jar thought it was time to jump out. So he asked in a soft tone, 'Is it time, Master?' thinking it was the leader outside.

Clever Marjenah replied in a manly voice, 'Not yet!' She had realised that the pack of thieves was hiding in the jars. She took the oil from the first jar, heated it and poured it in each jar, killing them one by one. From forty, the thieves were reduced to one.

When the leader threw out some stones as a signal, none of the thieves appeared. He was shocked to discover that they were dead. In anger, he left Alibaba's house and rode away to the forest.

The leader was devastated and decided to take revenge. So he came back to Alibaba's house as a silk merchant. Once more, Marjenah tricked the leader by pulling out the dagger hidden under the leader's silk garment and killing the last thief of the lot.

Alibaba was grateful to Marjenah for saving his life from the thieves and asked her to marry his only son. Alibaba was the only man left with the secret of the cave. He visited it after a year and found all the gold where it was. He finally shared the secret of the cave with his son and everyone lived happily.

Arabian Nights

Sindbad the Sailor

Indrani Vohra

Om KIDZ
An imprint of Om Books International

Once upon a time a porter named Sindbad got tired and hungry. He took a break to rest on the bench outside a mansion. He complained to God that it is unfair for some people to be poor while some enjoy the luxuries of life.

The owner of the mansion was a sailor, also named Sindbad. He heard the porter and reached out to him. The sailor told the porter that he was also poor once and all his wealth came to him because of his voyages. Sindbad the sailor then began the story about the adventures that made him rich.

Sindbad's father was a rich merchant who left him a small fortune which Sindbad spent entirely. He set out on a voyage so that he could recreate his wealth. With a bunch of other traders, he explored different lands. He bought and sold goods on every island, increasing his wealth, bit by bit.

One fine day, they reached the most beautiful island of them all. The sailors decided to take a break from their journey and began collecting wood to light a small fire to cook their food.

Suddenly there was a strong tremor and the ground began to move. The sailors realised that the island was actually a resting whale on which trees had grown. The whale dove deep into the ocean to destroy the fire and the sailors were pulled into the water.

Sindbad spotted a log and managed to hold onto it. He stayed afloat for a long time and tried to reach the ship with the sailors. By then the ship had departed. Slowly but steadily, Sindbad used that log and reached another island.

The island was ruled by a King Mirjahn. On reaching the island, Sindbad was extremely tired and hungry. He found some nuts, berries and fresh water. After quenching his thirst and hunger, Sindbad began exploring the island and found a mare.

He fed the mare some grass when suddenly, he saw a white sea stallion coming for the mare. He knew he had to act fast to save the mare. So he ran toward the stallion with a stick and scared it away.

The sea stallion immediately ran back into the waves from where it had come, never to return. A few minutes later, a man came up to Sindbad and asked him, 'Who are you?' Sindbad replied, 'My lord, I am Sindbad the Sailor. I would have drowned if I had not found a wooden log, clinging to which I have reached this beautiful island. May I know who you are?'

The man replied, 'I am one of the king's men. I look after his favourite mare who you just rescued from a monstrous sea stallion.'

The man then took Sindbad to King Mihrjan's court and reported to the king how Sindbad had saved his favourite mare. The king, thoroughly impressed with Sindbad, offered him a place in the court. Sindbad replied, 'Your Majesty, it will be an honour. I accept your offer humbly.' Thus, Sindbad became a master of the island's port.

One fine day, Sindbad saw the same ship that he had sailed on from his home visiting the island. The captain of the ship recognised Sindbad and embraced him. The captain said, 'Your goods lie safe in my ship.' Sindbad who had already risen in wealth in King Mihrjan's court offered some of the goods to the king.

In return, the king gifted Sindbad boxes filled with treasure and sent him sailing back. Sindbad sailed to another island where he sold some of his goods for tenfold the price and became richer. He returned home a rich man and started life afresh as a trader.

After narrating the story of his voyage, Sindbad the sailor asked Sindbad the porter, 'So now that you know about the hardships I had to go through to become wealthy, do you still think it is unfair that I have these riches?' The porter apologised to Sindbad the sailor and the two men became good friends.

Arabian Nights

The Enchanted Horse

Indrani Vohra

Om KIDZ
An imprint of Om Books International

Once upon a time, the people of Shiraz, Persia, were celebrating the New Year. The Sultan of Shiraz was sitting on his throne, watching his subjects celebrate, when he saw a man riding a wooden horse decorated with silk. The young man dismounted the horse and said, 'Your Majesty, I am an Indian and the owner of this horse which has magical powers. Sitting on its back, I can fly wherever I want to.'

The sultan replied, 'Prove your words. Fetch me a palm leaf from the tree on the mountain to the east.'

The Indian mounted the horse, turned a tiny screw located on its neck and flew off. A minute later, he reappeared on the horseback at the city square. He placed the palm leaf on the sultan's hand. The Indian kept the sultan amazed by showing him the flying skill of the horse.

The sultan decided to buy this horse. He asked the Indian, 'What price do you ask for this enchanted horse?'

The Indian replied, 'Your Majesty, I ask for your daughter's hand in marriage in exchange for this horse.'

The sultan smiled. But this reply angered his son, Prince Firoz. The sultan asked the prince, 'Why don't you ride the horse and see if it works well?' The prince mounted the horse and heard the Indian's instructions on flying the horse. But in haste, he didn't hear the instructions on how to stop it.

Once the prince flew off, the sultan got worried about his return. In anger he imprisoned the Indian and ordered to execute him if the prince did not return safe and sound.

Meanwhile Prince Firoz located the screw below the horse's ear and turned it in the opposite direction. The horse descended and landed on the roof of a palace. He peeped into the palace and saw a beautiful maiden lying asleep in bed. Mesmerised by her beauty, the prince instantly fell in love with her. As he approached the bed, the sound of his steps woke her up. She was taken aback. 'Please don't fear. I am the Prince of Shiraz. I seek your protection.' The maiden said, 'I am the Princess of

Bengal. You are my honoured guest.' She sent for her maids who took the prince to a guest room where he sought rest. The princess had fallen in love with him too. The next day, both admitted their feelings for each other and the prince told her about the enchanted horse. They sought the King of Bengal's permission and flew off to Shiraz. There, he put the princess up in a rest house.

The prince went to meet his father, the sultan, who was delighted to see him. He ordered the Indian's release. The Indian was free but wanted revenge. He went to the rest house and said to the princess, 'The sultan has sent me to fetch the Princess of Bengal.'

He mounted the enchanted horse with the princess and flew off. As soon as the prince got to know, he immediately began his search for her.

The Indian landed in Kashmir where the Sultan of Kashmir rescued the princess and killed the Indian. The sultan decided to marry the princess, who feigned madness so that the sultan wouldn't marry her. None of the doctors of Kashmir could cure her.

Meanwhile, Prince Firoz reached Kashmir and was elated on finding his love. He presented himself in the sultan's court as a learned doctor who could cure the princess. The Sultan of Kashmir told him, 'If you cure her, I will give you the wealth you want.' The prince on meeting the princess revealed his identity and together they devised an escape plan.

Prince Firoz went to the Sultan of Kashmir and said, 'Your Majesty, the only way to cure the princess is to make her sit on the enchanted horse as some of its magical powers have entered her body. I'll pour some magic potion on both of them. Arrange for the horse to be placed in the city square tomorrow morning and get the princess escorted there.'

The next day, everyone came to see the curing of the princess. On her arrival, the prince, dressed as a doctor, asked her to mount the horse. The prince lit a coal fire, stoked the coal with powder which caused smoke to rise. As the smoke grew thicker, the prince turned the screw on the enchanted horse and flew away with the princess.

The prince and princess reached Shiraz and had a regal wedding, living happily ever after.

Arabian Nights
The Fisherman and the Genie

Indrani Vohra

Om KIDZ
An imprint of Om Books International

Once upon a time there lived a fisherman with his wife and three children. He used to throw his fishing nets out in the sea every day. One day, he threw out the net only to find that he had caught a donkey. Surprised by this catch, he prayed to God for forgiveness as he thought this was the result of his sins. He threw his net a second time and caught a pitcher full of broken glass and mud. Once again he prayed to God for forgiveness.

When he threw the net for the third time, it brought back a golden jar covered with a lid. He knelt upon the sand and studied the jar. He stuck a finger inside but felt nothing. He turned it upside down but nothing fell out. Just as he was about to toss the jar back into the sea, a thick cloud of smoke formed and out came a genie!

The fisherman was in awe. 'Genie, how did you come to be shut inside this jar?' asked the fisherman.

'I shall grant you one thing,' the genie said, without answering his question. 'You may choose your manner of death.'

'Why would you kill me?' the fisherman asked in fright.

'Hear my story and you shall understand,' replied the genie.

'It began long ago, when I rebelled against the King of the Genies. To punish me, the king enclosed me in this jar and sealed it with a lid. That should have been bad enough, but then he flung the jar into the sea. For the first century of my captivity, I swore to honour the man who would release me with many riches. A century passed but no one rescued me.'

'During the second century of my captivity, I vowed to give all the treasures in the world to the man who would set me free. Another hundred years passed but no one came. In the third century, I swore I would make my saviour the king of the world, staying near him at all times, granting him three wishes each day. But another century passed

and I was still trapped in the jar. Filled with hopelessness, my anger grew so great that at last I vowed that whoever set me free would be punished with death; his only wish to be granted would be to choose the manner of his death. So you must choose,' the genie explained.

The fisherman understood that he needed to use his wits to get out of the situation, so he devised a plan. He said to the genie, 'Tell me genie, did you really live inside this small jar? It's hard to believe that this jar could contain even the smallest portion of someone as massive as you. I won't believe such a thing. It is impossible,' declared the fisherman.

'How dare you?' cried the genie out of anger. He began to transform again into smoke. He twisted himself into a spinning mass, tighter with every passing second and slid back into the jar. 'There!' he bellowed from inside, his voice echoing. 'Do you believe me now?'

The fisherman quickly put the cap on the jug and said, 'Now I shall toss you back into the sea and I will leave a warning to all fishermen who cast their nets here—never open a golden jar you find in these waters.'

'You tricked me!' the genie cried. 'Take off the lid. I promise not to harm you. I will repay you with tremendous wealth.'

The fisherman shook his head and said, 'I cannot trust you,' and tossed the jar into the sea where, people say, it still remains to this day.

Arabian Nights

The Ruined Man Who Became Rich

Indrani Vohra

Om KIDZ
An imprint of Om Books International

Once upon a time, there lived in Baghdad a wealthy man who had lost all his money and become so poor that he could barely afford a meal a day. One night, while he slept, he saw in his dream a man, who said to him, 'Your fortune lies in Cairo. Go there and seek it.'

The man went to Cairo. By the time he arrived, it was already evening. So, he decided to seek refuge at a mosque for the night.

The same night, a group of bandits entered the mosque and made their way into the adjoining house. The owners of the house heard them come in and cried out for help. The police came to their aid. The bandits ran away, but the police kept searching all over. They entered the mosque, and on finding the man from Baghdad, got hold of him and beat him up. They thought it was he who had tried to rob the house next door.

They put the poor man into jail. After three days, the police chief sent for him and asked him, 'Where are you from?' The man answered, 'I am from Baghdad.' The chief looked at him with a quizzical expression on his face.

'What brought you to Cairo?' He asked. The man replied, 'I saw a dream where a man said to me that my fortune lies in Cairo. So I came here to get it. But the fortune he had promised me turned out to be the generous beating you gave me!'

The chief laughed and said, 'O dear man, I have seen a dream thrice where a man said to me, "There is in Baghdad a house with a large courtyard and a garden that surrounds it. At the lower end of it is a beautiful fountain under which is buried a fortune. Go and get it." But I am wise enough to know it is just a dream.'

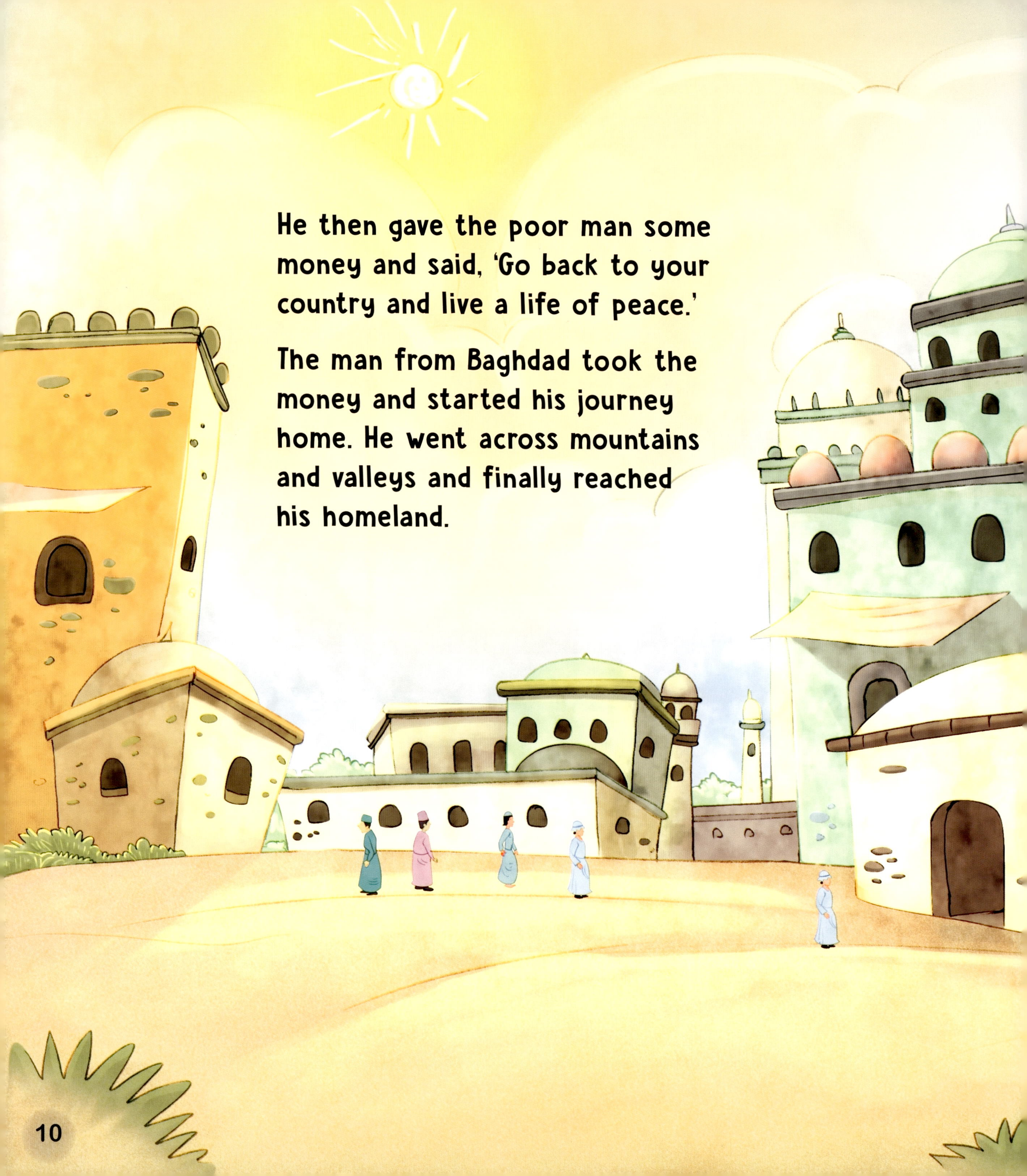

He then gave the poor man some money and said, 'Go back to your country and live a life of peace.'

The man from Baghdad took the money and started his journey home. He went across mountains and valleys and finally reached his homeland.

Now, the house in Baghdad that the chief had described belonged to the poor man when he was rich. The poor man thought, 'Why don't I dig underneath the fountain in my garden? Maybe there is a fortune in store for me.' He did so and to his utter surprise, there lay a treasure of gold under the fountain!

He couldn't believe his eyes! Finally, God had heard his prayers and bestowed him with wealth. With his newfound treasure, the man made a bigger house with a bigger garden. He bought a new horse for himself and endless gifts for the poor living in the city of Baghdad. The man was simply elated and now lived a life of comfort and joy.

He looked up towards the sky and thanked God for blessing him with this abundant fortune and a great destiny. He was, indeed, the ruined man who became rich again!